THE USBORNE BOOK OF STENCIL FUN

W9-BBY-846

Ray Gibson

Edited by Fiona Watt • Designed by Robert Walster

Illustrated by John Woodcock • Photographs by Howard Allman

Series editor: Cheryl Evans

With thanks to Freddy Hopf and Red Madrell
Stencil equipment provided by The Stencil Store Company Limited, Chorleywood, Hertfordshire, England.

Contents

Starting out

A stencil is a shape or design cut into cardboard or plastic to make what is called a 'stencil plate'. You then dab ink or paint into the cut-out shapes, leaving a pattern when the stencil is lifted off. You can brighten up all kinds of plain surfaces by decorating them with stencils, and in this book you will find lots of stencil templates to copy. Here you can see some of the equipment you can use and the first basic techniques you need.

Brushes

You can buy stencil brushes in many art or craft stores. They come in a variety of sizes, but a small one is ideal for the projects in this book. Always wash your brush after using it.

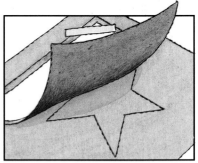

You can use a sponge or crumpled cloth to fill in a stencil. These give it an uneven, textured pattern.

You can buy special stencil paint in many craft stores.

Stencil paints

The paint you use needs to be quick-drying. Acrylic paint is ideal, but it can be quite expensive. Use poster paint or ready-mixed paints on paper, but you'll need to use fabric or acrylic paint on material and special ceramic paint for mugs or plates.

Transferring a design

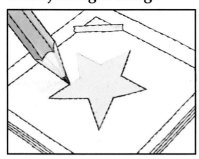

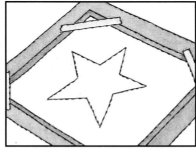

1. Carefully trace the outline of the template onto tracing paper or greaseproof paper. Use a very sharp pencil or a thin felt-tip pen.

2. Tape some carbon paper, inky side down, onto a piece of stencil cardboard. Add little pieces of tape to secure the tracing on top.

3. Go over all the lines with a ballpoint pen, pressing firmly. Peel off all the tape. Remove the tracing paper and the carbon paper.

Stencil plates

Most of the projects in this book suggest using stencil cardboard. This is oiled cardboard, sometimes known as oilboard, which you can buy from a craft store. You can also use any of the materials shown here. The holes you cut in a stencil are called windows and the parts between them are bridges.

Oil-based stencil crayons can give a very soft effect. Find out how to use them on pages 14-15.

This stencil is cut from special oiled manila cardboard or 'oilboard'.

The cut-out parts of the butterfly are windows.

The parts between the wings, head and body are bridges.

Clear book-covering film is ideal to use on curved surfaces and fabric.

You can use stiff paper but the paint makes it go very soggy quickly.

Some stores sell a special plastic, called Mylar®. It is expensive but it's very good.

To make thin cardboard last longer, rub a drop of cooking oil over both sides with a rag.

Cutting out

Always put a cutting surface beneath the stencil when you use a craft knife. Very thick cardboard is good or use a pile of old magazines.

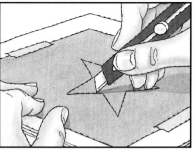

You will need a sharp craft knife. You can buy one from an art or craft store. Be very careful when using it. Always cut away from your fingers.

Cut out the smallest shapes first, then do the larger ones. Cut curved lines with short cuts rather than trying to do them with one long cut.

Using a stencil

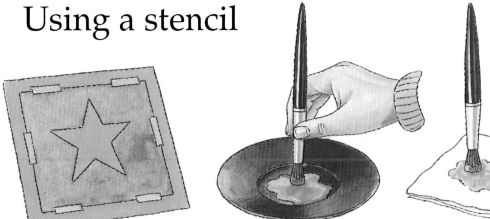

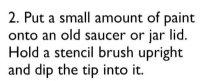

Test your brush on some scrap paper to check that it is not too wet.

1. Use little pieces of masking tape to attach your stencil firmly onto the surface you are going to decorate.

2. Put a small amount of paint onto an old saucer or jar lid. Hold a stencil brush upright and dip the tip into it.

3. You need hardly any paint on your brush when you stencil, so dab most of it off onto a kitchen paper towel.

Go over it again if you want to make a darker shade.

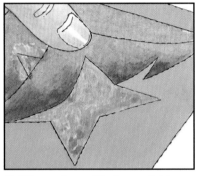

4. Dab the brush up and down firmly around the edges of the stencil. Fill in the middle of the stencil after doing the edges.

5. The paint will dry quickly, but wait a little while, then peel off the tape. Lift off the stencil very carefully.

6. Clean your brush well and leave it to dry. Wipe any paint off your stencil, dry it and store it flat in an envelope.

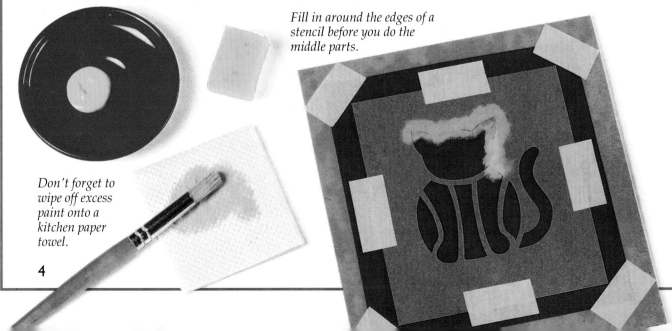

Fill in around the edges of a stencil before you do the middle parts.

Don't forget to wipe off excess paint onto a kitchen paper towel.

Tips and ideas

Window

If you make a mistake while you are cutting a stencil, put pieces of masking tape over the front and back of the cut, then trim away the extra tape.

Masking tape is good to use as it peels off easily.

You can also get fuzzy edges if the stencil moves while you are using it. Make sure you secure it firmly with tape to the surface you are decorating.

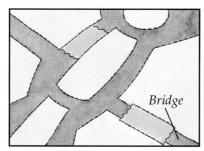

Bridge

To repair a broken bridge, tape the two ends exactly together on both sides of the stencil. Trim away the extra tape as neatly as you can.

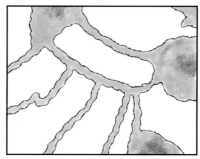

If you use a stencil several times, the edges get clogged with paint. Clean it with a damp cloth on both sides. Dry it well before using it again.

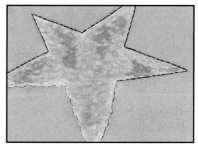

If you get fuzzy edges you have had too much paint on your brush. Your brush needs to be almost dry. Next time, dab it well on a paper towel.

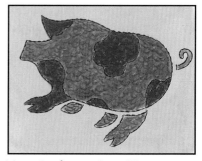

You don't need to fill in a window with just one shade of paint. You can add some different paint once the first one has dried.

Mix different paints together if you don't have the shade you want.

The shade of the paint you are using may change if you are working on a bright or dark background. Test the paint before you start.

To make an area darker, go over it again and again. Don't be tempted to put lots of paint on your brush, as you will end up with fuzzy edges.

5

Moon and stars card

You will need: stencil cardboard; stencil brush; stiff blue paper 20×14cm (8×5½in); masking tape; ready-mixed or acrylic paint; old saucer; kitchen paper towels; tracing paper; carbon paper; ballpoint pen; thin felt-tip pen; glue stick.

To fill in a square card, add extra stars around the edge of your main stencil.

Gold or silver paint looks good on dark paper. Mount the stencil onto gold paper then glue it onto a card.

1. Lay a piece of tracing paper over the template on page 32 and secure it with tape. Trace the lines with a thin pen.

You could stencil stars onto the front and flap of an envelope.

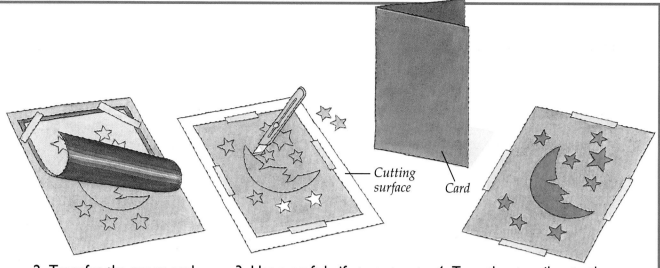

Cutting surface

Card

2. Transfer the moon and stars onto stencil cardboard using carbon paper and a ballpoint pen (see page 2).

3. Use a craft knife to cut out the stars, then the moon. Fold the paper for the card in half, with the short sides together.

4. Tape the stencil onto the card. Make sure that none of the windows overlaps the edge. Tape both to a work surface.

5. Dip the tip of your brush into some paint and dab it on a paper towel. Stencil the edges of the moon. Fill in the rest.

6. Stencil all the stars, making sure that you press the brush carefully into all their points. Leave the paint to dry.

7. Peel the tape off the stencil and carefully lift it off the card. Wipe both sides of the stencil before using it again.

Different ways of filling in

To make a shaded moon, dab paint around the edge of the stencil. Gradually fade out the painted area leaving the middle part completely bare.

For a textured look, dip a scrunched-up paper towel or a sponge into some paint. Dab it on another paper towel then dab it over the stencil.

Dab household glue (PVA) onto the stencil with a paper towel, then lift the stencil off. Sprinkle glitter onto the glue and shake off any excess.

Mugs, plates and bowls

In most craft stores, you can buy a special kind of ceramic paint which you can use on china. You usually bake it in an oven to make it permanent.

You will need: one or two shades of ceramic paint; plain ceramic (not plastic) mug; black felt-tip pen; ruler; clear book-covering film; masking tape; scissors; ballpoint pen; old saucer; kitchen paper towels; sponge; scrap paper.

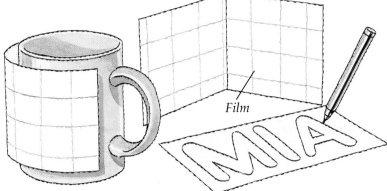

Film

1. Cut a piece of book-covering film the same height as the mug and long enough to fit from one side of the handle around to the other.

2. On scrap paper, write a name in fat letters with a black pen. Make sure it fits the film. Fold the film in half, short sides together.

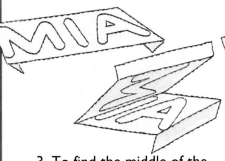

Middle part

3. To find the middle of the name, fold the paper over at the edge of each outside letter. Then fold the piece of paper in half.

4. Tape the film over the letters, lining up the middle fold of both the tracing and the film. Trace around the letters with a ballpoint pen.

5. Place the film on a cutting surface. Cut out all the letters with a craft knife. Keep any middle parts of the letters, as you will need them (see right).

Peel off the backing paper.

Add any middle parts of letters.

Before sponging, fill in any gaps with tape.

6. It's tricky to put the letters on as a strip, so cut between them. With the handle facing you stick the first letter to the right of it. Add the others.

7. Put paint onto the saucer. Dip the sponge into it, dab it on a paper towel then over the letters. When it is dry, you could dab on another shade.

8. Peel off the film carefully when the paint is dry. Carefully follow the manufacturer's instructions for hardening the paint.

Use a small stencil around the edge of a bowl.

You could use a stencil from another project in this book. For the cat and the moon templates see page 32.

Middle parts of letters

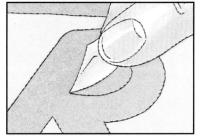

Cut out the middle parts of letters, such as A, D, and O, before you cut around the edge. Add the cut-out piece to complete the letter.

Letters to copy

ABCD
EFGHI
JKLMN
OPQR
STUV
WXYZ

Snazzy socks and shoes

You will need: a pair of socks; cardboard; stencil cardboard; masking tape; kitchen paper towel; fabric paint or acrylic paint; old saucer; scissors; tracing paper; stencil brush; pencil; carbon paper.

If you use fabric paint, use cotton socks, not man-made ones, as you usually need to 'fix' the paint with a warm iron. Acrylic paint can be used on man-made fabric as it doesn't need to be 'fixed'.

1cm (½ in)

1. Lay one sock on a piece of cardboard and draw around it, leaving a 1cm (½in) margin. Cut out the shape.

2. Put the shape inside the sock to stretch it flat. Tape this onto another piece of cardboard.

3. Trace any small template and transfer it onto stencil cardboard (see page 3). Cut it out and tape it to a sock.

4. Put paint on the saucer. Dip the brush into it, then onto a paper towel. Stencil the edges then the middle.

Stencil by dabbing up and down.

Stencil a matching sock in the same way.

5. Go over the paint again to make it bright. Let the paint dry then peel off the stencil. Repeat around the sock.

Tie your shoes with bright laces.

You could decorate matching socks and shoes in contrasting shades.

Canvas shoes

Clean the rubber and eyelets with a damp cloth.

1. Trace a design onto stencil cardboard and cut it out. Stuff scrunched-up newspaper tightly into the shoes.

2. You could paint a pair of shoes with bright acrylic paint. Leave them to dry before decorating them.

3. Tape your stencil onto the shoe. Using the same method as for the socks, fill in the stencil with acrylic paint.

4. Peel the stencil off the shoe. Let the paint dry. Clean the stencil before using it again in a different place.

Small stencils to trace

Piggy T-shirt

You will need: stencil cardboard; craft knife; ruler; masking tape; different shades of fabric paint or acrylic paint (including white); small pieces of cloth; stencil brush; several old saucers or clean plastic tubs for mixing paint; pins; washed and ironed cotton T-shirt; large piece of cardboard 1cm (½in) wider than the T-shirt; clean scraps of paper; kitchen paper towels.

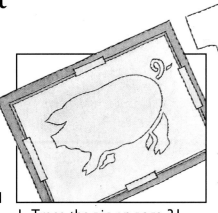

Push the pin through the top layer of the T-shirt only.

1. Trace the pig on page 31 onto stencil cardboard. Also draw the border around it. Cut out the stencil then trim around the border.

2. Find the middle of the T-shirt by folding it in half exactly. Mark the middle by putting a pin at the top and bottom of the fold.

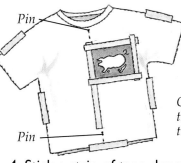

Pin

Pin

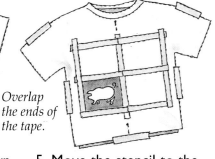

Overlap the ends of the tape.

3. Open out the T-shirt and push the cardboard inside. Make sure that the material is smooth. Tape the T-shirt onto your working surface.

4. Stick a strip of tape down the middle of the T-shirt, lining it up with the pins. Place the stencil next to the strip and add three strips around it.

5. Move the stencil to the other side of the middle strip and add three more strips around it. Add two more boxes below in the same way.

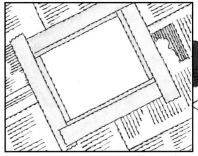

6. To avoid getting paint in the wrong place, surround the top left-hand box with pieces of scrap paper. Secure the paper with tape.

7. On one saucer, mix one shade of paint with a little white. Bunch up a dry piece of cloth and dip it into the saucer. Dab it onto a paper towel.

8. Dab paint all over the box. Remove the scrap paper and put it around another box. Fill that one in with a different shade of paint. Repeat.

To stencil the pig

1. Tape the stencil exactly over one of the boxes. Use the brush to stencil the pig in a deeper shade. Build up the paint gradually (see page 5).

2. Carefully remove the stencil and clean it. Repeat with the other three boxes. Peel off all the masking tape when the paint is dry.

To make a frame

You'll find the stencil template for the cat on page 32.

For a small child's T-shirt, stencil one pig in the middle.

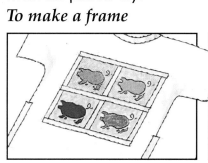

1. Stick strips of tape around the outside of all the boxes, following their edges exactly. Trim the tape to make sure that the corners meet.

2. Add two more rows around the outside, carefully lining up the edges of the tape. Pull off the middle row of tape to leave an even gap.

3. Tape paper around the edge and in the middle to protect the T-shirt. Use cloth dipped into paint to fill in the gap, as before. Dry. Remove the tape.

Outer space

You could stencil this scene from outer space on the wall in your room, but make sure that you ask permission first. If you don't want to stencil directly onto a wall, use a large piece of paper and hang it as a poster. These stencils were filled in with special stencil crayons from a craft store, but you could use poster or stencil paint instead. Plan your design before you begin.

You will need: yellow and white oil-based stencil crayons; stencil cardboard; craft knife; tracing paper; pencil; carbon paper; masking tape; kitchen paper towel; two stencil brushes - or just one, but you will need to clean between each shade. To clean the brush, soak it in white spirit or paint thinner in a jar, then wash it in soapy water and dry it well.

1. Fold the tracing paper in half. Tape it over the half-planet below. Trace it then turn it over and draw over the lines to complete the shape.

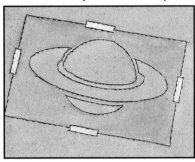

2. Use carbon paper and a sharp pencil to transfer the planet onto the cardboard and cut it out. Use masking tape to attach it to the wall.

3. Rub the yellow crayon very hard onto a pad of paper towels to break the seal. Rub it onto another part of the pad to make a patch of crayon.

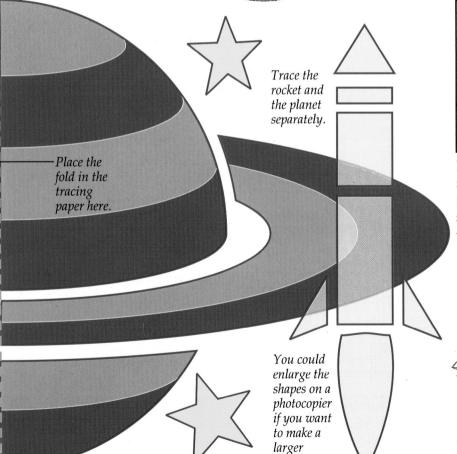

Place the fold in the tracing paper here.

Trace the rocket and the planet separately.

You could enlarge the shapes on a photocopier if you want to make a larger stencil.

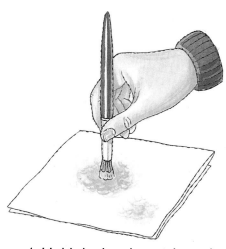

Cut curved lines to make the tail of a shooting star.

4. Hold the brush upright and work the bristles around and around in the patch on the paper towels. Continue until the tip is covered in crayon.

Design your own rocket by drawing around objects.

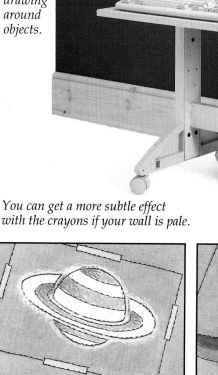

5. Fill in the yellow bands with the same circular movement. Add more crayon to your brush and go over it again if you want a deeper shade.

You can get a more subtle effect with the crayons if your wall is pale.

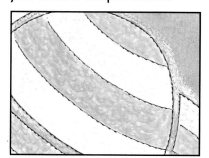

6. Cover the tip of a clean brush with white crayon. Fill in the other bands. If your wall is dark you may have to go over it to make it show up.

7. Use the yellow crayon to add a little shading to the edge of the planet and ring. You could use a darker shade of yellow or orange.

8. Peel off the tape and the stencil cardboard. Try not to touch the finished stencil for a day or two until the crayon completely dries out.

Design your own stencil

These pages show how to make a stencil from your own drawing or from a picture or photograph. They also show how to fill in a stencil with different shades of paint.

You will need: a bold, clear picture; tracing paper; pencil; masking tape; ballpoint pen; craft knife; saucer; kitchen paper towels; brush or sponge; carbon paper; stencil paint; stencil cardboard; eraser.

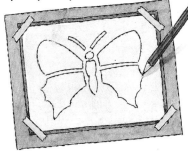

1. Tape tracing paper over the picture. Draw around the main shapes with a sharp pencil. Try to avoid drawing any tiny shapes.

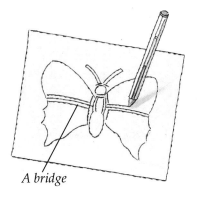

A bridge

2. Peel off the tape and remove the tracing paper. Draw bridges to separate each main shape. Don't make them too narrow.

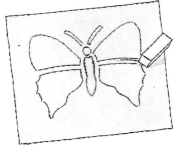

3. Use the ballpoint pen to draw carefully around each main shape of the butterfly. Erase all the pencil lines which run along the bridges.

4. Make a second neat tracing of all the outlines. Transfer the shapes to stencil cardboard using carbon paper and a sharp pencil. Peel off all the tape.

5. Cut out the stencil using a craft knife. Use a brush or a sponge to fill it in. Follow the steps below if you want to use different shades of paint.

Adding different shades

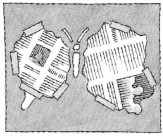

1. Use masking tape to cover small windows or scrap paper on larger ones. This will stop any paint from going through when you dab it on.

2. Fill in the uncovered windows with one shade of paint. Allow to dry. Make a light pencil mark at each corner of the cardboard.

Match the corners with the pencil marks.

3. Cover the windows you have painted. Put the stencil back in place matching the corners. Tape down and fill in. Allow to dry and remove.

Always iron the clothes on the wrong side after washing them.

See page 11 for instructions on how to decorate shoes.

Sweatshirts and leggings

You could stencil your own design onto clothes, but always ask permission before you do. **You will need:** kitchen paper towels; sponge; acrylic paint; book-covering film; old saucer; cardboard.

1. Cut cardboard slightly wider than your leggings or sweatshirt. Push the cardboard inside and tape it to a work surface.

2. Trace a stencil onto the back of book-covering film. Cut it out. Peel off the backing and press it onto the fabric.

3. Dip a sponge into some paint on a saucer. Dab it onto kitchen paper. Fill in the stencil. Peel the stencil off the fabric when dry.

17

Snowman window

You will need: stencil cardboard; tracing paper; carbon paper; craft knife; masking tape; saucer; white poster paint; sponge; kitchen paper towels. **For the snowflakes;** large plate; thin white paper; scissors; ruler.

Ask for permission before you stencil on your windows. The paint will wash off with detergent and water when you want to remove it.

1. Trace the snowman on page 31 and transfer it onto stencil cardboard (see page 2). Cut it out with a craft knife.

2. Make sure the window is clean and dry. Tape your stencil to it. Make sure the tape doesn't cover the holes.

3. Put some white paint onto a saucer. The sponge needs to be dry so if yours is damp, squeeze it tightly in a cloth.

The sponge gives a snowy effect.

4. Press the sponge into the paint. Dab off any excess paint on a paper towel, then dab the sponge over the stencil.

When the paint is dry, scratch a face with a pencil.

5. Leave the stencil in place for a few seconds to dry. Carefully peel off the tape and remove it from the window.

A row of snowmen

Mark the position of the stencil before you move it.

Masking tape

Previous position of the stencil.

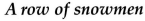

1. Put a strip of tape along your window. Tape the stencil to the middle of the strip. Stencil with a sponge.

2. Mark the corners of the stencil on the tape. Move the stencil along, lining it up with one mark. Stencil again.

3. When you get near to one window frame, go back to the middle and stencil the other half of the window.

Different shades

Add different shades of paint by masking out the holes you don't want to stencil with scrap paper (see page 16).

For a very snowy effect, sponge the tree with green paint. When dry, dab a little white paint over the top of it.

Snowflakes

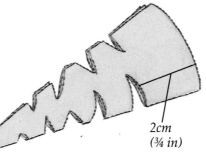

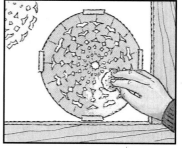

1. Draw around a plate onto thin paper. Cut out the circle and fold it in half four times, creasing well.

2. Leaving 2cm (¾in) at the curved edge, cut out shapes. Open it out and tape it onto a window. Sponge with paint.

2cm (¾ in)

3. Move the stencil and sponge it again. You can only use paper stencils a few times as they get soggy.

Embroidered fish cushion

You will need: 35cm (14in) square cushion pad; 2 pieces of cotton cloth 40cm (16in) square; medium wadding or batting 40cm (16in) square; Mylar® (see page 3); waterproof pen; stencil brush; craft knife; needle; pins; scissors; embroidery needle and threads; thin thread; masking tape; old rag; kitchen paper towels; ruler; acrylic or fabric paints; stiff cardboard.

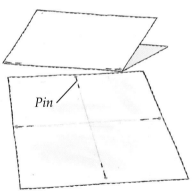

1. Fold one cotton square in half from top to bottom. Put a pin to mark the fold. Open out and fold the other way. Pin in the same way.

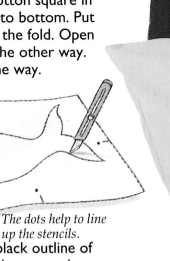

2. Cut two pieces of Mylar® 25cm x14cm (10in x 6in). Mark the middle of each side. Tape a piece over the fish on page 22. Line up the marks and the dots.

3. Trace the black outline of the fish with the pen and mark in the dots. Remove the tape and cut around the outline. This is stencil **A**.

The dots help to line up the stencils.

4. Tape on the other piece of Mylar®. Trace the blue outline of the eye, lips, fins and scales. Peel off the tape and cut them out. Add the dots. This is **B**.

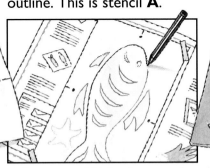

5. Put stencil **B** back onto the template exactly in place and tape it down. Trace the black outline of the fish onto it but do not cut around it.

6. Tape the pinned piece of cotton flat onto the cardboard. Tape on stencil **A**. Line up the bottom of the stencil with the pins at the sides.

Line up the top and bottom dots with the pins.

You could also stencil starfish or shells onto the back of the cushion before you sew it together.

It's a good idea to plan your design on paper before you begin.

If you use a bold shade of cotton, test your paints on a scrap to see if they show up.

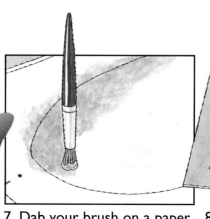

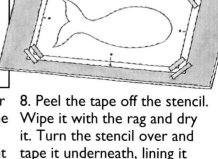

7. Dab your brush on a paper towel, then stencil around the fish. If you want a shaded effect, gradually fade the paint into the middle.

8. Peel the tape off the stencil. Wipe it with the rag and dry it. Turn the stencil over and tape it underneath, lining it up with the pins. Fill it in.

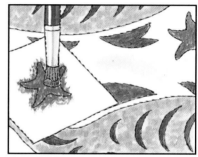

9. Tape stencil **B** on top of the first fish, lining up the outlines exactly. Stencil over and over the shapes until you get a deep shade of paint.

10. Trace the starfish and the shell onto Mylar®. Cut them out. Stencil them around the fish. If you have used fabric paint, iron the fabric to 'fix' it.

To embroider the cover

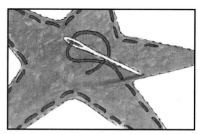

1. Lay the decorated square on top of the wadding making sure that the corners match. Use pins to secure the two layers together.

2. Thread the needle with thin thread and tie a knot. Stitch around the square, about 2cm (¾in) from the edge. Use long tacking stitches.

3. Using the embroidery thread, sew around the shells, fish and starfish. Stitch in and out through both layers. Use stitches about 5mm (¼in) long.

Continues on the next page

Embroidered fish cushion: continued

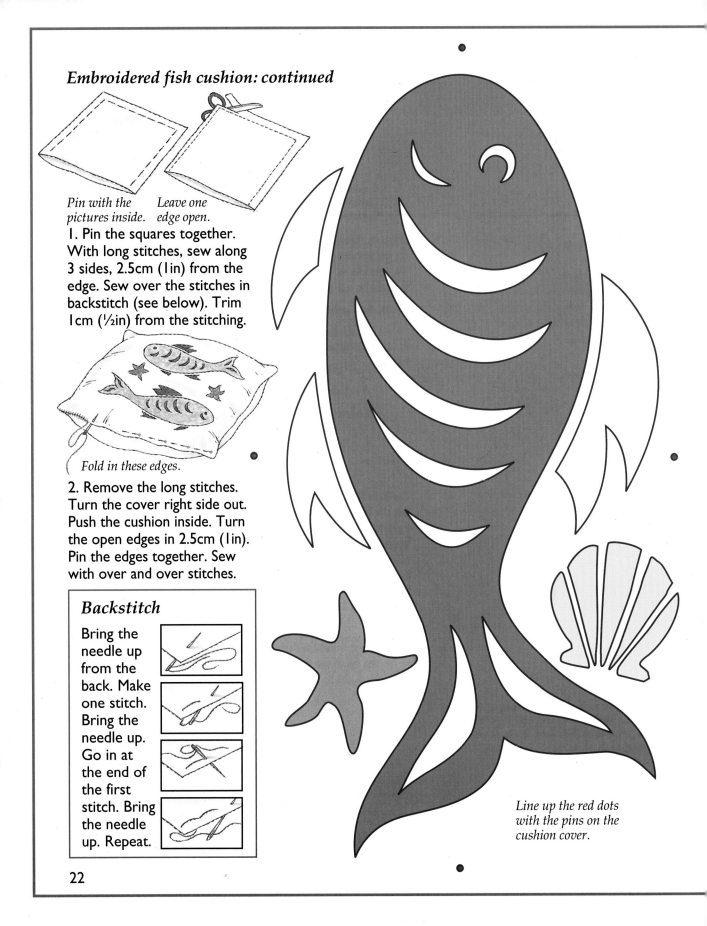

Pin with the pictures inside.   *Leave one edge open.*

1. Pin the squares together. With long stitches, sew along 3 sides, 2.5cm (1in) from the edge. Sew over the stitches in backstitch (see below). Trim 1cm (½in) from the stitching.

Fold in these edges.

2. Remove the long stitches. Turn the cover right side out. Push the cushion inside. Turn the open edges in 2.5cm (1in). Pin the edges together. Sew with over and over stitches.

Backstitch

Bring the needle up from the back. Make one stitch. Bring the needle up. Go in at the end of the first stitch. Bring the needle up. Repeat.

Line up the red dots with the pins on the cushion cover.

Body stencils

You will need: water-based face paint (from a toy store or theatrical supplier's); tracing paper; small piece of sponge; craft knife; clear book-covering film; carbon paper; ballpoint pen; clean rag; masking tape.

1. Trace the template. Transfer it to the paper side of the book-covering film, using carbon paper.

2. Tape the film onto a cutting surface. Use a craft knife to cut around the outline of the stencil very carefully.

3. Dampen the sponge, then wrap it in the rag. Squeeze it very hard to get out as much water as possible.

You'll find the templates for the bat and the skull on page 31.

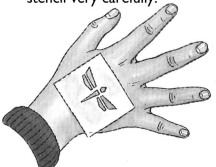

4. Carefully peel the film from its backing paper. Stick it in place on a patch of clean, dry skin. Smooth it down all over.

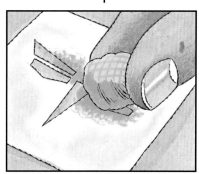

5. Rub one side of the sponge in the face paint. Dab it over the stencil, gradually building up the paint.

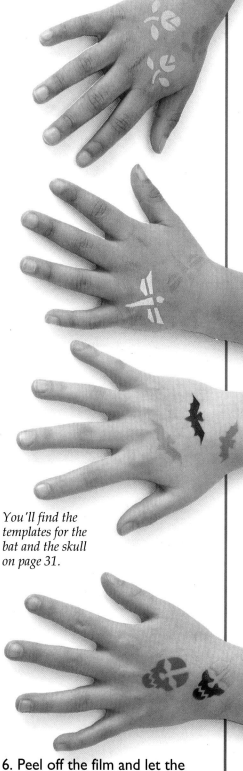

6. Peel off the film and let the stencil dry. When you want to remove the stencil, wash it off with soap and water.

23

Fat cat gift wrap

You will need: stencil cardboard; carbon paper; ballpoint pen; masking tape; craft knife; stencil paint or acrylic paint; stencil brush; old saucer; kitchen paper towel; large sheet of paper to decorate, such as tissue paper, plain gift wrap or brown paper.

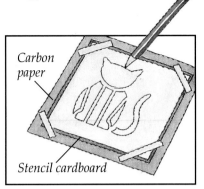

Carbon paper

Stencil cardboard

1. Trace the cat template on page 32. Transfer the design onto stencil cardboard, using a ballpoint pen and carbon paper (see page 2).

2. On a cutting surface, cut out the eyes, whiskers and nose, then the whole head in one piece. Keep it to one side. Cut out the cat's body.

If you are decorating tissue paper use a double layer.

3. Tape the paper you want to decorate onto a flat, dry surface. Tape the large stencil of the cat's body onto one corner of the paper.

Dry the brush on a paper towel.

4. Put one shade of paint onto a lid. Stencil around the outline with a very dry brush (a wet brush will wrinkle the paper), then fill in the middle.

5. When the paint is dry, place the head back in position on the stencil. Stencil the eyes, whiskers and nose in another shade of paint.

Decorated cats

Add stripes in different shades. Do some with a stripy tail and body.

Add patches in a different shade once the first shade has dried.

Go over the tips of the ears, the tail, the paws and the cheeks to deepen the shade.

Use dark paint on gold or silver paper for a stunning effect.

For a gift tag, stencil onto cardboard and cut around it. Make a hole and add some ribbon.

Erase the pencil lines when you have finished.

To decorate a whole sheet of gift wrap, move the stencil, when dry, to another position and fill it in. Try placing it at a slant or even upside down.

To stencil rows of cats, rule faint pencil lines every 12cm (5in). Stencil in the same way as the snowman border at the bottom of page 18.

Trace the little mouse on page 32. Transfer it onto stencil cardboard and cut it out. Stencil it in the large spaces between the cats.

Folder and bag

The folder is decorated with a reverse stencil, where the paint goes around a cut-out shape leaving an outline, instead of filling in a window. **You will need:** a folder about 32×24cm (12×9in) when closed; pencil; carbon paper; old toothbrush; tracing paper; scissors; craft knife; masking tape; stiff paper; pencil; acrylic paints; saucer.

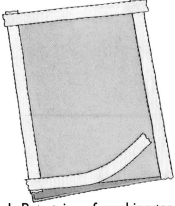

1. Put strips of masking tape along each side of the front of the folder. Make the tape overlap at the corners.

2. Trace the seafloor template on page 32. Transfer it onto stiff paper using carbon paper and a sharp pencil. Cut it out.

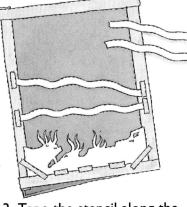

3. Tape the stencil along the bottom of the folder. Cut some wavy lines from stiff paper and tape them on.

4. On the saucer mix some acrylic paint with a little water until it is the consistency of runny cream.

5. Cover an area with newspaper. Place a can or a box to prop up the folder at an angle in the middle of it.

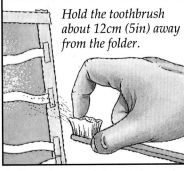

Hold the toothbrush about 12cm (5in) away from the folder.

6. Dip the toothbrush into the paint. To spatter the paint, flick your fingernail toward you along the bristles.

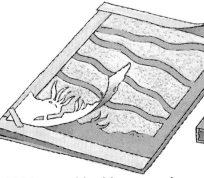

7. You could add a second shade of paint once the first one is dry. Peel off the tape and the stencils when dry.

8. Transfer the fish on page 32 onto stencil cardboard. Cut it out. Tape it onto the folder and fill it in with a stencil brush.

You can decorate cardboard or plastic objects with a personal design so that they are easy to identify.

You may need to trace the seafloor template more than once to fit around the bag.

Bag stencils

You will need: all the things for the folder; bag; book-covering film; sponge; kitchen paper towels.

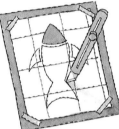

Use book-covering film for all the stencils on the bag.

1. Trace the templates onto the back of book-covering film. Cut them out carefully with a craft knife.

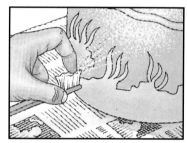

2. Peel the backing off the seafloor stencil and press it along the base of the bag. Spatter as before.

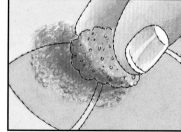

3. Use a sponge to stencil some fish between the wavy lines. Peel all the film off the bag when the paint is dry.

27

Gifts and other ideas

You can make lots of gifts even more special or more personal by decorating it with stencils. Most of the ideas on these pages use stencils from this book, but you could design your own (see pages 16-17). Before you begin, make sure that the stencil will fit onto your gift. Also check that you are using the right kind of paint. Acrylic paint is suitable for most surfaces, including fabric, wood and paper.

Terracotta pots

To decorate a terracotta pot, follow the instructions on page 8, but use acrylic paint rather than ceramic paint to fill in. Once the paint is dry, it becomes waterproof.

You'll find the fish template on page 32, the dragonfly on page 23 and the flower on page 11.

You can buy a plain bright kite from a toy store or a kite store.

Kite

Cut a stencil from stencil cardboard and fill it in with acrylic paint, using either a sponge or a brush. Lift off the stencil when the paint is dry and move it to another place.

Mouse mat

Buy a plain computer mouse mat and design your own stencil to put onto it (see page 16). Use cardboard for your stencil and fill it in with acrylic paint and a sponge or stencil brush.

The shell and the starfish templates are on page 22.

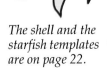

Writing paper

Buy some writing paper and envelopes. Tape a cardboard stencil in the same place on each sheet of paper. Fill it in with a brush and a contrasting shade of paint.

Storage boxes

Plastic surfaces can be decorated using acrylic paint. Cut your stencil from cardboard or book-covering film. Use a sponge to apply the paint.

The turtle template is on page 11 and the shell is on page 32.

Eggs

You can stencil the surface of hard-boiled eggs with food dye and a sponge. Boil the eggs first and allow them to cool. Use a small stencil cut from book-covering film.

There are other small templates on pages 11 and 23.

Photograph frame

You could liven up a photograph frame with lots of bright stencils. Cut your stencils from stencil cardboard and use acrylic paint and a sponge to fill them in.

Baseball cap

Cut a small stencil from book-covering film. Press it on and fill it in with a brush and acrylic paint. It's a bit tricky to fill in some parts. Try putting the cap over an upturned bowl.

The template of the star on the baseball cap is on page 31.

29

Candles

You will need: water-based paints such as acrylic paints (do not use oil-based paint); candle; masking tape; piece of sponge; stencil cardboard; craft knife; kitchen paper towel; tracing paper; carbon paper; old saucer; pencil.

Tree template

Striped candle

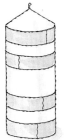

You don't have to make the spaces between the tape exactly the same.

1. Wrap strips of masking tape around the candle. Leave spaces in between. These will be the painted parts. Put some paint onto a saucer.

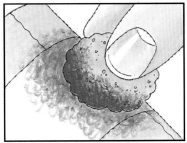

2. Dab the sponge into the paint then onto a paper towel. Fill in the spaces between the tape. Allow to dry, then add a second coat. Remove the tape.

Tree candle

Trace the tree template and transfer it to stencil cardboard using carbon paper. Cut it out then tape it onto the candle. Dab the paint on with a sponge.

You could use any small stencils to decorate candles (see pages 11, 28, 29 and 31).

Follow the instructions on the left of the page to add a stripe around the bottom of the candle.

Templates

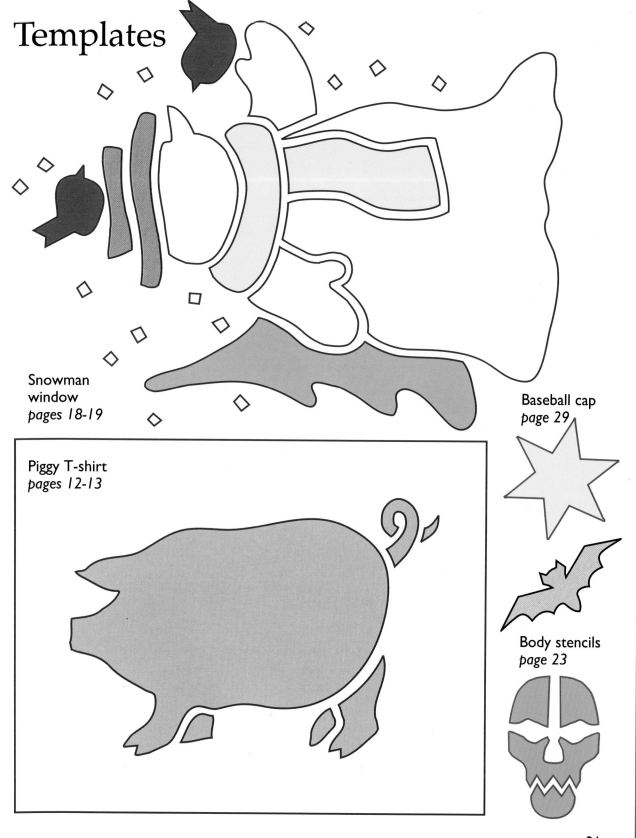

Snowman
window
pages 18-19

Piggy T-shirt
pages 12-13

Baseball cap
page 29

Body stencils
page 23

Seafloor
pages 26-27

Moon and stars
pages 6-7

Fat cat and
mouse
pages 24-25

32